NAKED BUNYIP DANCING

STEVEN HERRICK

pictures by Beth Norling

ALLEN&UNWIN

ect has been assisted by the Commonwealth G
alia Council, its arts funding and advisory body

Council
for the Arts

ished in 2005

Unwin
der St
st NSW 2065

1 2) 8425 0100
2) 9906 2218
o@allenandunwin.com
w.allenandunwin.com

ibrary of Australia
g-in-Publication entry:

teven.
yip dancing.

114 655 0.

hildren – Juvenile fiction. I Norling, Beth.

text illustrations by Beth Norling
text design by Sandra Nobes
Bembo by Tou-Can Design
Australia by McPherson's Printing Group

5 4 3 2

s Billy has said this term' was published in *E*
ol Magazine, March 2003

war poem' was published as 'Early Monday
Sand, New Writing on War and Peace, Frances

This pro
the Austi

Australia

First pub

Copyrigh
Copyrigh

Allen & U
83 Alexan
Crows Ne
Australia
Phone: (6
Fax: (61
Email: in
Web: ww

National I
Cataloguir

Herrick, S
Naked bur

ISBN 1 74

1. School c

823.3

Cover and
Cover and
Typeset in
Printed in

10 9 8 7 6

'Wise thing
NSW Scho

'Mr Carey'
Lines in the

Michael

It's the same every year.
38 degrees in the shade
as we trudge back to school,
thinking of the beach
and the long days swimming
and hanging out,
wearing what we like,
eating when we like,
doing what we like,
and now...
Mum even ironed my uniform!

I'm walking along the scorching bitumen
with Peter,
who can't stop talking
about how much he ate
on Christmas day,
and how many presents he got,
and where his family plan to go
for holidays next year,
and as he says that,
he stops,
and it hits him.

Next year is
a long time away
from where we are now,
walking through
a blistering summer
going back to school.

Our new teacher

Mr Carey has long hair,
and a beard.
He wears flared trousers,
and beads,
and a T-shirt with the slogan
'Meat is murder' on the front,
and 'McDonald's = McJunk' on the back.
Today is his first day.
He plays us music
by someone called
Bob Dylan,
who sounds like
he swallowed a bag of marbles
and got two stuck up his nose.
Mr Carey closes his eyes,
raises his arms,
and sings along
with Mr Dylan.
The whole class
is nervously quiet,
watching.
When the bell rings
no one moves.

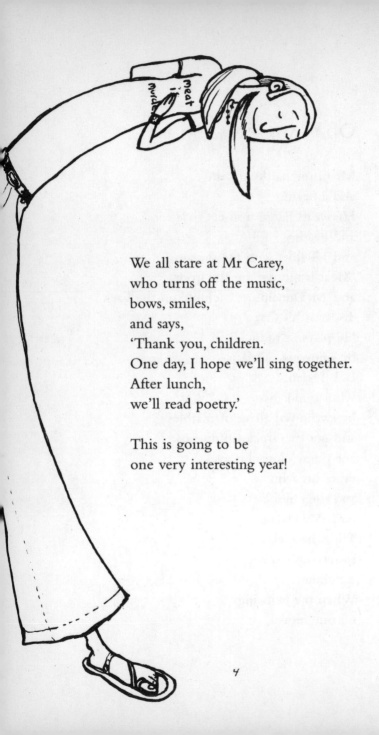

We all stare at Mr Carey,
who turns off the music,
bows, smiles,
and says,
'Thank you, children.
One day, I hope we'll sing together.
After lunch,
we'll read poetry.'

This is going to be
one very interesting year!

Nicknames

Mr Carey, the madman – Sophie
Carey, the crooner – Anna
Carey, the scary! – Ahmet
Marble nose! – Me!
The beaded one – Jason
The bearded beaded one – Emily
Mr McDonald's – Alex (who loves hamburgers)
Mr Vegetarian – Sarah (who hates hamburgers)
The tofu butcher – Peter (no, I don't get it either)
Mrs Batlow, come back – Rachel (who liked our
    last teacher)
Mrs Batlow, come back – Sean (who didn't like
    our last teacher!)
Carey, the hairy – Billy

We all look at Billy
and together
we nod
and say
in a whisper,
'Carey, the hairy.'

Poetry, after Lunch

At least Mr Carey
didn't make us write
a boring essay on
'what we did on our holidays'
so he can't be too bad.
He read us poetry
and some of it was okay,
and he didn't try to teach us
about images and metaphors
and similes.
I hate similes!
Our old teacher always used to say,
'A simile is when you say
something is like something else.'
We'd all laugh at old Mrs Batlow
with her grey hair and granny glasses
saying this was like that,
and we were like this,
all the time, *like*,
she was sounding like Jessica Simpson!

Mr Carey read aloud,
and he asked us what we thought.
At first, no one raised their hand.
We weren't sure what to say,
then, finally,
Peter said he liked the one on food,
Sarah said she liked the animal poem,
Ahmet liked the football poem,
but when Mr Carey asked Billy
which poem he liked,
Billy,
who had been staring out the window,
quick as a flash, said,
'I liked the poem on punk music.'
Mr Carey looked confused.
'I didn't read a poem on punk.'
And Billy smiled
and said,
'Exactly.'

Billy

I think Mr Carey
smiled at my punk joke.
I'm sure
underneath all that beard hair
I saw a slight upturning
of the lips.
Could we have a teacher
with a sense of humour?
I thought they went out of fashion
along with beards and Bob Dylan!
But I'd be willing to put up with poetry,
and awful Mr Dylan,
if it meant we could have a laugh.

Alex, on holiday?

I'm sure glad Mr Carey
didn't ask us to write
about our holiday.
How do you write an essay
on helping your dad move out
to go and live in a little flat
around the corner?
And spending half the time
sitting in the bedroom
listening to your parents
argue
over what Dad can take
and what has to stay behind?
And every argument ends
with one of them saying,
'As long as Alex is happy.'
That's when I put the pillow
tight over my ears
so I couldn't hear any more
and so I wouldn't shout,
'I'm *not* happy!'

I spent exactly twenty days
at Dad's place,
and twenty days
at our house with Mum,
which I think is my parents' idea
of being fair and even.

I couldn't wait for school to start.
How weird is that?

The J-man

I'm Jackson Jacobs – the J-man.
Coolest kid in the land.
New in school.
Ain't no fool.
Jacobs the name – call me Jackson.
Rappin's the game if you want satisfaction.
Got sunglasses – yeah.
Got a beanie – yeah.
Baggy pants – baggy, yeah.
Walk with a carefree lope.
Ain't no nerdy dope.
I'm so cool I'm a refrigerator.
Hear me sing, excitement generator.
Talk in rhyme.
Yeah, all the time.
Jackson – the J-man.
Wish I was American.
But I'm new in school
and I'm from Dubbo.
Don't go to Dubbo
no no
no Dubbo
nothing rhymes with Dubbo
so I gotta go.
Remember me, I'm free.
I'm Jackson – the J-man.

The class respond to the J-man

Cool
— Sarah.
Ice, baby, ice.
— Isabella.
Great shoes. Skate shoes.
— Alex.
Are they long pants or short pants,
or long shorts?
— Billy.
Is Dubbo in America?
— Emily.
Is Dubbo in outer space?
— Jason.
Can he make a rhyme with orange?
— Me.
Do we call him Jackson, or the J-man?
— Sophie.
I can't understand a word he says.
— Mr Carey.
I think he's on drugs.
— Sean.

I think he's on red cordial.
– Peter.
Why is he wearing a beanie in summer?
– Ahmet.
I like him.
– Jessica.
I still can't understand a word he says.
– Mr Carey.
Welcome J-man!
– Anna.

I think they like me!
– the J-man.

Michael's secret

Emily and Jason
have done it.
They've kissed.
Yeah – lips,
open mouth,
spit and teeth everywhere.
I saw them.
Like two question marks
facing each other –
joined at the top.
Emily loves Jason,
and so does Jason
I reckon.
Soon it'll be all round
the whole school
unless
we keep quiet about it.
That's why
I'm only telling
you

and Peter

and Anna

and Billy

and…

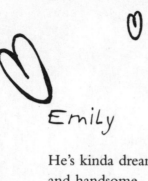

Emily

He's kinda dreamy,
and handsome.
He's like Brad Pitt
in *Troy*,
only he doesn't wear a dress.
He's quiet,
but that's okay.
He listens.
And he kisses like
he kisses like
he kisses like…
Well.
He kisses good.
Okay!

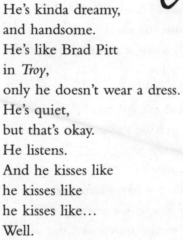

Jason

She thinks I'm handsome!
And she says I look like Brad Pitt
but without the dress.
I hope she's not imagining me naked!
She talks a lot,
but that's great
because I don't say much.
And I'm getting the hang
of this kissing thing.
It's kinda nice –
I mean it's not like playing soccer,
or eating lots of ice-cream,
or going to the movies on the weekend,
but,
like I said,
it's kinda nice.

The Principal welcomes our new secretary

Good morning, children.
Welcome to our Monday assembly.
There are a lot of messages today.
I expect you all to listen quietly
and I thank our new secretary,
Mr Jonesforthwalton,
for compiling this list
so quickly this morning.
Welcome to our school Mr J-F.

Sport is cancelled on Wednesday
because girls are advised
to wear hairnets in cooking class.
The canteen is offering sushi at lunchtime
and the winner gets a holiday to the Gold Coast.
The school raffle has a few tickets left
and remember the prize
is a Maths Competition after school.

Ms Park, the Year 5 teacher, warns everyone
that there are angry magpies nesting
in the trees near the oval,
so please
be careful of the bus passes in force from Monday.
The office staff will only issue late passes
to boys riding skateboards in the girls' toilets.
Finally,
the two teachers caught kissing behind the gum trees
by those children from Year 4
are advised that next time
their parents will be informed
and detention is a certainty.
Newsletters will be posted on Tuesday,
and those items will be
confiscated and destroyed.
I'm away for the rest of the day,
and Class 2K will be in charge.
Any questions?

Michael converts to yoga

Mr Carey's okay.
The first week of Bob Dylan
and poetry
was bizarre,
but we all like
the yoga exercises
every morning.
Except Billy
who gets so tangled up
it takes three of us
to untie him.

And the J-man
has written a rap about Mr Carey.
    He's way-cool weird
    Long black beard
    Trousers mighty lairy
    That's our Mr Carey.

Alex drew a picture
of Mr Carey.
Here it is…

He's probably not
as handsome as this,
but he's okay.
We like him.

Anna, quiet and still

It's worth it,
all the untangling of Billy,
for the fifteen minutes of yoga
every morning
when we sit
cross-legged
on the mat
and we practise
thinking of nothing,
letting our minds go blank.

When Mr Carey
first told us that,
Peter laughed so hard.
'Let my mind go blank?
I'll get an A for this,
no worries.'

And it works!
We sit
lotus position
every morning
and all I hear
is my breathing
and all I see
is gentle darkness
as I close my eyes
and turn my brain
to stand-by
and drift…

We sit
quiet and still…

until Peter farts.

The boy with the talking bottom

I can't help it.
Okay?
My bottom has a mind of its own.
And it speaks at the worst times.
In exams.
At the dinner table,
but only if we have guests.
On planes.
At a wedding once,
right before the bride said 'I do.'
I think my family stopped
going to church when I was young
because of my 'problem'.
Mum even took me to a doctor.
Can you believe it?
He said I should eat more fibre,
whatever that is.
Dad says it's nervous tension.
I reckon my bottom and I
don't like long silences,
and one of us just has to speak.
And yoga?
Fifteen minutes of silence.
What do you expect will happen!

Billy's yoga

I thought Mr Carey said
he's going to teach us 'Yoda'.
You know,
the little guy from *Star Wars*?
I've always wanted to be
a Jedi Master,
so I went along with
the body contortions
and the exercises
and the meditation,
hoping against hope
that Mr Carey had special powers.
It's not that I believe
everything I see in the movies.
But my dad told me
that when the government
asked the population
what religion they were,
700,000 people wrote
'Jedi Masters'.
So anything is possible,
I guess.

Then Anna told me it was *yoga*,
not yoda.
I still try the exercises,
but I get so twisted up
I think my body wants
to be a Jedi Master,
not a Yoga Master.

Michael's quiet Lunch

Six of us boys
and three of them girls
sit on the school fence
at lunchtime
waving at the cars.
(Well, waving at the drivers
and passengers anyway.)
No one waves back.
Some are singing along to the radio,
or slyly picking their noses,
or
they stare straight ahead,
lost in dreams.
Billy *meows* at a dog in a ute.
The dog barks and growls.
A boy in a big black Mercedes
makes a rude hand gesture
and gets nine rude hand gestures back.
Another boy pokes his tongue out.
We ignore him.
We're not childish.

Then a semitrailer storms by.
We all yank the air,
blowing imaginery horns,
hoping...

The big bearded truckie
lets rip.
Hoooooooonnnnnnnkkkkkkkkk!
It's so loud
it knocks Billy off the fence!
We all laugh
and run back to class,
yanking the air,
yelling,
Hooooooonnnnnnnkkkkkkkkk!

Co-curricular activities

Co-curricular activities?
No, we don't know what it means either.
Mr Carey says it's stuff you do
on Friday afternoons
and you don't have to do tests
or be marked on it.
You do it for fun!
And he's taking suggestions:
J-man: Rap singing, sir, and dancing.
Ahmet: Soccer, cricket, golf
and swimming in summer, sir.
Sarah: Tree planting.
And learning about the environment.
Frogs, lizards, birds and fish!
Billy: Climbing trees, sir.
Me: And falling out of trees!
Emily: Belly dancing, sir. But only for girls.
Jason: Ballet dancing, sir. But only for boys!
Billy: Naked Bunyip Dancing, sir. But only for
bunyips!

Anna: Yoga. Lots of yoga.

Peter: Yoghurt. Yoghurt making, sir.

Alex: How about co-curricular ice-cream eating, sir?

Mr Carey crosses his arms and frowns.

'Class 6C, please keep your suggestions sensible.'

Billy replies: Truck driving, sir!

Truck driving for children.

Alex: Advanced butchery, sir.

Peter: Farting for beginners, sir!

Now the class is giggling so much,

we can't help ourselves.

Frog throwing.

Car demolishing.

Navel gazing.

Stargazing.

Daytime stargazing!

Head shaving for children.

Head shaving for teachers!

Mr Carey touches his ponytail,

gingerly.

Billy says,

'Tadpole squashing, sir. Advanced tadpole squashing!'

All the class laugh.

Even Mr Carey.

Alex, any day of the week

Saturday afternoon I go to Dad's place,
until Monday.
Monday morning I catch the bus to school
and home to Mum's in the afternoon,
where I stay until Wednesday,
when Dad picks me up from school
and I stay at his place that night
because Mum has her late class
at university.
Thursday, it's back to Mum's
until Saturday,
when I wait for Dad
with a bag
overloaded with books and clothes,
and things I might need
because Dad hasn't bought everything
for his little flat yet.
Mum and Dad try to humour me
and they talk
in really fake excited voices
about how I'll have two of everything soon.

Two bedrooms
two beds
two televisions
and maybe even
two computers
if Dad gets the promotion at work.

And I can see they're serious about all this.
Two of everything,
but only one parent at a time.

Mr Carey announces an excursion

Good morning, students.
Tomorrow is our first excursion
for the year.
We'll be sharing the day with Class 5P.
Ms Park and I
have had long, spirited conversations,
enjoyable conversations,
animated conversations
on where we should go.
Yes, the beach was mentioned.
And the zoo.
I think you'll all be *very* surprised
with our final choice.
And can I say
that the destination was influenced
by a member of this class.
Someone who,
what's the word I'm thinking of...
broadcast,
loudly broadcast
a possible location.

Anna and the excursion

Great!
An excursion!
The first one of the year.
The zoo?
The beach?
The zoo and the beach?

What!
Where?
The Sewerage Works!
Well, I hope the sewerage *works*,
but we're not going there,
are we?
To see sewerage?
That stinks!
Yes, I know it stinks,
but I mean it stinks
that we're going there
and not to the beach.
Why?
For a class assignment
on the environment.
The beach is an environment, isn't it?

To see where waste goes.
We know where it goes:
down the dunny
(or on Dad's lemon tree,
when he's a little drunk).
Why don't we study waves?
Or tides.
Seashells. And sand.

Two dollars.
Two dollars!
We have to *pay*
to go to the Sewerage Works.

It stinks!

Michael on the excursion

If I pinch my nose
and close my eyes,
hold my breath,
put my fingers in my ears,
don't move,
don't touch anything,
and think
only fresh-air thoughts
about
clean surfing waves
and pure white sand
and an ice-cream
with chocolate topping
well…
well…
I'm still
at the Sewerage Works
and it still stinks.

Or, as the J-man says,
'Stunk stank stinky stunky,
who you calling smelly flunky?
stunk stank stinky stunky,
smells like a dead
smells like a dead
smells like a dead donkey!'

Billy and the excursion

I thought it was cool.
I agree with Dad –
no one knows where stuff goes.
We flush
and think it disappears
into the centre of the earth
and stays there
with the dinosaur bones
and oil deposits
for millions of years.
How many people live in the world?
Billions.
And most flush,
at least once a day.
And if it did just disappear into the earth,
imagine
it expanding
as time goes on
getting bigger and smellier
deep down,
until one day –

one sweltering hot day
in the middle of summer
when the earth's core
can't take it any more –
it just explodes!

So I'm glad we went
on the excursion.
It might not have been
as much fun as the beach,
but
now we know
that sewerage helps the earth.
It feeds the soil
by decomposing.

I can't wait until class tomorrow.
During Maths
I'm going to raise my hand –
you know,
toilet time –
and I'll say,
'Mr Carey?
Can I go fertilise the planet?'

School Rules!?

BE POLITE TO FELLOW STUDENTS.
And rude to the teachers.
WEAR A HAT OUTDOORS.
Go naked indoors!
NO BULLYING ALLOWED.
Do it quietly instead.
ADDRESS THE TEACHERS AS 'SIR' OR 'MISS'.
Call Mr Carey 'miss'
and Ms Park 'sir'.
SWEARING WILL NOT BE TOLERATED.
It will be encouraged!!
GRAFFITI IS STRICTLY FORBIDDEN.
Unless you sign your name!

Peter — the graffiti-artist?

Every year
someone graffitis
on the School Rules.
It's always a laugh
to hear Billy read it out to everyone
before Mr Corrigan,
the school cleaner,
comes along and scratches them off,
swearing under his breath
that next year
he'll set up a video
and catch the culprit.

And rumours sweep
the schoolyard
that it's me.
Every year:
'Peter did it!'
or
'It looks like Peter's writing.'

I'm cool.
I don't mind the gossip
because I know
no one can prove it,
and I also know
everyone wishes
they were the secret
graffiti-scrawler.
Everyone
except Mr Corrigan,
who stares at me
extra closely
as he carries the bucket
back to his shed.

Billy and poetry

I can't get this poetry thing.
Mr Carey
asks us each to write one.
He says write what you think.

I think nothing.

Write how you feel.

I feel stupid.

Describe your day.

Too much poetry!

Your weekend.

No poetry!

Does it rhyme?

NO!

Is it happy?

It's a poem!

Is it sad?

It's a poem, okay?

Loud?

YES! VERY LOUD!

Quiet?

No way!

So, Billy.
What is your poem about?

*IT'S A LOUD PUNK
POEM ABOUT NOTHING!*

43

Sophie's alternative poem...

Our teacher's name is Mr...............
Carey, Smith, Barnacle

He lives on.................. Road
Dawson, Pearce, Toad

He rides his.................. to school
bicycle, motorbike, donkey

leaving it locked at the..................
gate, shed, dentist

At lunch, he always eats a..................
sandwich, pie, cockroach

and drinks two bottles of his favourite
....
cola, juice, chilli sauce

Most afternoons the class sit
and listen to him read..................
books, newspapers, toilet paper

We laugh and giggle, especially
when he tells us about the...................
old man, child, goldfish-eating spider

For sport, he always wants to do.....................
cricket, soccer, bungee jumping

He waves us home as we board the ,................
bus, train, elephant

As we leave, he shouts,
'Don't forget, tomorrow is..................
exam day, an excursion, a turnip

Class 6C at cricket practice

I'm a pace bowler.
   I'm an opening batsman.
I'm a spinner. Yeah, like Warnie.
   I'm a wicket-keeper.
I'm an all-rounder.
   I'm going to be in big trouble
   when I get home. I've lost my batting gloves.
I'm a swing bowler.
   I'm fast. Fast as the wind.
I'm an off-spinner.
   I'm captain.
I'm better than Lleyton Hewitt.
Oops. I'm at the *wrong* practice.

I'm the coach.
Who wants to bat first?

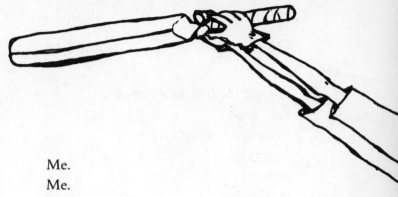

Me.
Me.
Me.
Me.
Me.
Not me. I've lost my gloves.
Me.
Me.
Me.
Me.
Me.
Me. Can I use my tennis racquet?

Peter's magic fingers

I've got the ball on a string.
I'm magic.
I can bowl off-breaks,
leg-breaks,
zooters,
wrong-uns.
The mystery ball is no mystery to me.
I can turn it at right angles.
The flipper?
Easy.
I'm Shane Warne.
I'm Stuart McGill.
I'm Mulith…
I'm Mullith…
Thanks Mr Carey, yeah,
I'm Muralitharan
the Sri Lankan spinner – he's great.
I'm a demon bowler.
A batsman's nightmare.
A winner.
Legend.
Hero.

Turn off my PlayStation, Mr Carey?
Play cricket, in the sun?
Me?
Sorry, sir.
I'm allergic to sport.

Billy asks Mr Jonesforthwalton a question

Can I have a late note, please?

No. I'll give you one immediately.

1

Music, with Ms Libradore

Good morning, Class 6C.
We'll start today's class with piano.
Can anyone play piano?
Anyone?
No, Billy. Not the drums,
the piano.
Yes, Sophie.
I'm sure Billy is very good on the drums,
but I don't see any drums in class,
do you?
Yes, Billy.
You *could* use the desktop as a drum,
but not right now.
We're learning piano today.
Yes, Michael,
we could use the desktop as a piano,
but why?
We have a piano here,
right beside me.
What do you think this big black thing is?
A coffin?
Very funny, Alex.

What, Emily?
A glory box full of wedding presents?
No, it's a piano.
Yes, Peter.
A piano would be a very silly place
to put wedding presents,
but there are no presents in this piano.
No. Nobody stole the presents.
There weren't any in the first place!
No, I don't know who's getting married.
And yes, getting married and not receiving a present
would be very sad, Emily,
but no one is getting married,
and no one is not getting presents.
What?
No one is not getting presents means
someone *is* getting presents, Sarah?
Well, yes. It does.
But it's not what I meant, is it.

First, we'll learn about keys.
And before anyone makes a stupid joke
about keys and locks and doors,
I've heard them all before, okay?
Let's start with the key of C.
No, Billy. You can't see C.
C is a sound.
A is a sound.

B is a sound.
C, A, B.
No, not cab,
not taxi!
Keys!
The key of C.
The key of A.
Listen.
C.
A.
B.
Any other keys?
No, Z is not a key.
Y is not a key.
They are letters of the alphabet.
Yes, like A,
but A is a key.
Oh, very funny, Billy.
A is A-key,
I see the joke.
Achy Breaky Heart
Now would you please stop singing
that stupid country music song!

I give up, Class 6C.
Forget piano.
Yes, Billy.
We'll do drums next lesson.

Michael and Maths

Mr Carey has a weird way
of teaching.
Take Maths.
(I'd like to take Maths
and throw it off a cliff!)
For Maths,
Mr Carey asks twenty questions
every morning,
just to 'refresh the memory'
as he likes to say.
Only the questions aren't
'What is 84 divided by 4,
multiplied by 5?'
Mr Carey's typical question is:
'If Collingwood kick 20 goals,
and 4 behinds,
what's their score?'
or
'If Australia beat New Zealand
58 to 56 in netball,
how many points were scored,
in total?'

When Mr Carey first asked
that question about Collingwood
we were all so surprised
no one had the answer.
So Billy, who goes for the Sydney Swans,
put up his hand and replied,
'If Collingwood kick 20 goals,
the answer, sir, is:
IT'S A MIRACLE!'

The class meet Sharita

It's Friday afternoon.
Co-curricular.
Mr Carey stands onstage,
a broad smile creasing his face
as wild rhythmic music
pounds from behind the curtain.
Flutes,
thumping drums,
floating whistles
and wailing vocal howls.
We look at one another.
What's happening back there?
Snake charming?
Camel racing?
Trapeze artists flying across the stage?

With a flourish
Mr Carey opens the curtain
to reveal
Sharita the Belly Dancer
and her band
(actually, a CD player).

She shimmies
and shakes
and wiggles
and belly rolls
across stage
as Mr Carey claps in time
and calls out,
'Welcome, Class 6C,
to Co-curricular belly dancing.'

Sarah and belly dancing for beginners

It's fun!
True!
Sharita,
whose real name is Sally
(and she's Mr Carey's sister),
shows us each a special move.
Peter does the camel walk,
complete with suspicious noises.
Ahmet is an expert
at the Turkish hip lift.
He thinks it will help his soccer.
Anna loves temple hands and snake arms.
She says it's like noisy yoga.
The J-man becomes expert
at the Egyptian hip drop,
which he calls
'the Egyptian hip-hop!'
But, best of all
are the zills –
little cymbals we wear on our fingers
and we click in time with the music.

Billy wears them on every finger
and even straps some to his toes.
He invents 'punk belly dancing',
although
it's a bit much
when he lifts his shirt
and tries a belly roll,
a shimmy
and a zill dance
all at the same time!

Alex's empty suitcase

On Sundays,
my dad and me
go to a football match
and eat a hot dog
and chips.
We drink thickshakes,
caramel, double ice-cream.
Sometimes we go to the zoo instead
and laugh at the monkeys
pulling faces at us.
I take a photo
of Dad in front of the gorilla.
In summer
we go to the beach:
boogie boards
and sandcastles,
frisbees
and kites.
Once we went to the museum
and saw dinosaur bones
and butterflies from New Guinea
in a glass case.

On Monday,
when Dad dropped me at the bus
after a Sunday
playing cricket in the park,
he asked,
'Where would you like to go
next Sunday?'
I thought of everywhere we've been
in the months since Dad left,
and I said,
'I'd like you to visit me,
at home,
and stay...'
Dad looked sadder
than an empty suitcase
and said,
'We'll go the beach,
will we?'

A concert? A play?

After a few weeks of co-curricular
with belly dancing,
guitar playing,
singing,
and Mr Carey's special acting lessons,
half the class
want to stage a concert
with music and singing,
and dancing.
The other half
want to do a play,
especially Emily,
who wants to do
Romeo and Juliet.
No prizes for guessing
who plays the lead.
Mr Carey doesn't mind,
so he suggests a vote,
after lunch.
A secret ballot to decide.

Michael does a quick count...

At lunch,
Emily offers everyone
a role in *her* play.
She's got 14 students,
including herself,
who'll vote for a play,
and 14 students
who'll vote for *anything* but the play!
The bell rings
and we all head back to class,
deadlocked!

We each write our choice
on the special ballot papers
(Mr Carey's yellow Post-it notes),
and wait
while Mr Carey counts.

Everyone's sure it'll be 14–14,
but the smile on Mr Carey's face says
there is a result...

He stands
and announces,
'Concert: 15 votes
Play: 13 votes.
It's a concert!'

Class 6C are stunned.
We look at each other,
everyone whispering,
'It wasn't me.'

Emily

If I find out
who voted for the concert
when they promised me
they'd vote for a play –
where Jason
could have been Romeo
to my brilliant Juliet –
I'll make them pay!

And I had the perfect plan
to win a recount tomorrow.
I was going to
download a photo
of Johnny Rotten
off the internet.
How ugly is that!
And I'd scrawl a signature
across the bottom.
I was going to give it to Billy
first thing
to make sure he changed his vote.
He'd do anything
for a Rotten autograph!

But somebody voted different
to what they said.
Jason looked so
disappointed.
To help him feel better
I'll get him to dance with me
in the school concert.
Me and Jason,
and ballet.

Peter the host

I'm not stupid you know,
no matter what everyone thinks.
As soon as we decided
on a school concert
I put my hand up
to volunteer,
and I acted heaps eager.
'Please Mr Carey,
please can I be the host?
I'll do my best, sir.'
The whole class
was so surprised
they all joined in.
'Come on, sir.
Let Peter do it.'
Mr Carey had to say yes.
Too easy.
I'm the host.

Do I want to be the host?
Well,
the real question is:

do I want to hide away
until the last minute,
avoiding any part in the concert
until someone gets sick,
or Mr Carey realises
that I don't have a role...
and suddenly
I'm forced to dress
in some stupid costume
being ordered to sing
or dance.
Or sing *and* dance!
No way.
So, I got in early.
I chose the simple role.
All I do is stand up
and announce the next fool –
sorry,
announce the next performer!

Sophie and poetry

I waited until the end of class
and I went to Mr Carey's desk
and asked him
in a really quiet voice,
in case anyone was outside listening,
if I could read a poem
in the school concert
instead of singing.
A poem of my own
on any topic I like.
He smiled so wide
I thought his face would split!

Simple.
And I've got months to write it!

Jason's secret

Think about it,
for just a minute, okay?
Emily wants a play.
Emily wants to be Juliet.
I'm Emily's boyfriend.
Who do you think
would have to play Romeo?
Hours and hours of rehearsal
in our dusty old school hall
when I could be outside
playing football,
or riding my bike
down to the shops,
and just hanging out.

It was a simple choice really.
And yes, I feel bad
about letting Emily down,
but
onstage
in front of the whole school...

I shiver at the thought.

The Rap Master ducks for cover

I'm a mean mother
a rapping brother
like no other
duck for cover
because here I come – the J-man.

I got nerves of steel
that's how I feel
I'm hyper-real
you get the deal
because here I come – the J-man.

Don't get in my way
or you're gonna pay
hear what I say?
scared, me? no way
because here I come – the J-man.

Here's the school gate
don't care if I'm late
everybody can wait
because I'm great
that's right, yeah – I'm the J-man.

Pupil-free day?
Teachers only today?
No way!
Oops.
No, I'm cool.
Hey, I'm the J-man.

Mr Carey tells us about his first game of football

I was nine years old
when a bigger boy
came up to me on the school oval
and said,
'You're okay.
You wanna play soccer?
My dad coaches for a club.
You should join.'
That afternoon
I ran home faster than
a winger with the ball at his feet.
'Please, Mum.
Can I join?
Brian's dad will take me. Please?'
All afternoon. Please, Mum.
Dinner. Please, Mum.
Dessert. Pleeeeeease, Mum.
YES!
I put on my old sandshoes,
shorts and t-shirt,
and ran to Brian's place.

He took me to training,
where I met all my team-mates,
including a kid who looked like a duck.
Everyone called him 'Duck'.
All night, under lights,
kicking a ball,
yelling 'Pass, Duck.'
Or my favourite,
'Shoot, Duck, shoot.'
They told me I needed
soccer boots
shin pads
team socks –
white with two green hoops –
all before Saturday,
and my first game of football.

'Please, Mum, please.'
Endlessly, all week.

Saturday.
Sunshine.
I rode my bike
six kilometres to the field,

wearing new boots,
new shorts, new socks,
and my shin pads
strapped to my arms
like a skate warrior.
(To this day, I don't know why
I put them on my arms,
not my legs.)
Our coach gave me
the number 8 jersey
and said,
'Play up front,
pass the ball
and help out in the middle.'
I ran non-stop,
tackled,
yelled,
dribbled,
and yes, passed,
and passed,
and passed.

Thirty-four years later
I remember
one pass...

The ball came to me
fast.
I trapped it with the instep
of my shiny new shoes.
I dribbled it a few paces
and when a defender
came in for the tackle
I passed the ball
just out of his reach
to Duck,
who kicked it smack bang
into the goal.
Everyone ran to Duck
to shake his hand
and pat him on the back.
I jogged back to the half-way line,
thinking
this is the best fun
I've ever had in my life.
And passing the ball
is the best thing
a kid could do,
ever!

Peter tells us about his first game of football

It was 0-0
with two minutes to go.
My team was shattered,
worn-out, beat, dog-tired,
whacked, helpless
and fading fast!
I got the ball
on the half-way line.
I controlled it perfectly
on my thigh,
brought it down with a neat flick
and jinked past the Italian defender.

           'What?'

I sent a delightful through ball to Ronaldo

           'Who?'

running down the touchline.
He did a one-two with Emerson,
the Brazilian midfielder,

         'Brazilian?'

and sent a driving low cross
to the near post,

where I dived full-length
to head the winner,
with seconds left.
The Italians were devastated
as my Brazilian team-mates
lifted me high on their shoulders...

      'Peter.'

and carried me into the stands...

      'Peter.'

as the samba played loudly...

      'Peter.'

and where the World Cup...

      'Peter.'

was presented to me by the Queen...

      'Peter!'

Yes, sir?
'Sorry, to interrupt the Queen,
but were you playing your X-box
last night?'
Oh no, Mr Carey.
It was last year
when I won the World Cup.

An autumn poem by Billy

the leaves are gently falling
like the steady flakes
of dandruff
when I haven't washed my hair.

A spring rap by the J-man

It's spring. It's spring.
Shake your shiny bling.
It's spring sing the birds
whistling without words.
It's spring shouts the king
who lives in Beijing!
It's spring, yo, it's spring.
Let those funky words ring.

A summer poem by Peter

Holidays.
Beach.
No school.
Enough said.

A winter poem by Emily

'Now is the winter of *my* discontent'
when dear Romeo and sweet Juliet
are forsaken
by yonder class...

who chose a stupid concert instead!!!!!

Michael's broken remote control

Dad slumps in his armchair
with the big blue cushion
behind his big bald head.
Mum relaxes on the lounge
where she can put her feet up –
her soft lilac slippers
warming her long pink feet!
My big sister Stella
sits on the lounge with Mum.
She plonks her feet on the coffee table,
and wiggles her smelly toes.
I'm forced to sit on the cushion
on the floor
in front of the telly.
Dad says,
'Michael, turn up the volume, will you?
You're closest.'
I lean forward and turn it up.
Mum says,
'Darling, it needs more colour.
Fix it will you? That's a good boy.'
I adjust the colour.

Now everyone on television
has faces pinker than Mum's feet.
Stella says,
'Dad, the picture's all fuzzy.
Everyone's got two heads.'
And sure enough,
Dad says to me,
'Just move the aerial, son.
Just a little, to the right.'
I get up,
move the aerial,
fluff my cushion to get comfortable,
ready for *The Simpsons*,
when
there's a knock at the door,
and Mum says,
'Visitors.
Turn the telly off, Michael.
There's nothing on anyway.'

Questions Mr Carey has not answered, yet.

Mr Carey, if the earth revolves around the sun,
and the moon revolves around the earth,
why don't they crash into each other?

Sir, if you can grow a beard on your face,
why can't you grow a beard on your elbow?

Mr Carey, why is there an aeroplane
called the 'Sopwith Camel'?

Mr Carey, why can't men get pregnant?

Why can't we see the hole in the ozone layer?

Why can't you grow a beard on your knee?

Why does Dad snore and wake everyone,
except himself?

Why can't you grow a beard on your bottom?

Class 6C answer a question

'Class 6C.
What do you call someone
who doesn't eat meat?'

A feral!

Poor?

A vegetablarian.

A meat-free zone?

A long-haired, tree-hugging,
good-for-nothing, layabout hippie.
(That's what my dad says, sir.)

An anti-carnivore.

A cow!
(Well, they only eat grass, don't they, sir?)

A cool salad dresser,
Sees animals as no lesser.

A brussel sprouter!

A tofu-burglar!

A soy-beaner!

Can we go now, sir?
It's lunchtime,
Meat pies and sausage rolls,
a dollar each!
If we're late,
Year 5 will get them all!

Anna's secret

Emily and Jason
have kissed again!
Before school,
on the bus,
up the back.
I couldn't watch.
Yuk!
So I watched!
Yuk!
Peter
Ahmet
Michael
Billy
Sarah
Alex
we all watched.
It was worse than
Big Brother.
Worse than *Survivor*.
Worse than *Australian Idol*.
So we watched.

No one's secret any more...

Emily and Jason
can't stop kissing!
True!
This time they did it
in the classroom
before study
when they thought Mr Carey
wasn't around.
He was!
Now, they've really done it...

Emily

I can't believe it!
Detention.
For kissing.
What will Mum say?
I've never got detention in my life.
How can Mr Carey do this?
Especially after I explained
Jason and I were in love.
Doesn't he always sing songs
about 'make love, not war'?
What a hypocrite!

Jason

I can't believe it!
Emily told Mr Carey we're in love!
And I got detention,
for kissing!

I've got detention before –
for breaking a school window,
for swearing,
for fighting.
But for kissing...
how embarrassing!

Alex's Saturday Soccer

It's the same every Saturday
now soccer season has started.
Mum stands on one sideline
watching my game,
drinking her coffee
and looking nervous.
Dad stands on the opposite side
shuffling his feet,
drinking his coffee
and watching Mum
from way across the field.
When the final whistle blows
I wait
in the centre-circle,
afraid to go one way
or the other.

Michael's weekend treat

It's the first meal
on the first night
of our first camping weekend ever.
Mum, my sister Stella
and me are sitting outside the tent
watching Dad
trying to put together
the brand-new twin-burner deluxe gas stove
for our first meal
on our first night...

'If I place this here,
screw this in,
tighten,
stand it on level ground,
and light...
Anyone got a match?'

I can't resist.
'Sure, Dad. A match.
How about Stella and a horse!'
'Very funny, Michael,' says Dad.
'You can apologise to Stella
by washing up tonight.'
Stella smiles and keeps reading
her stupid fantasy book.

'A match, please?'
Mum hands a box to Dad and says,
'I'm starving. Let's cook.'
Dad strikes the match,
talking to himself,
'Here we go,
a delicious dinner coming up.'
He holds the match close to the gas cooker
turns the knob, and...
nothing.

'It's broken!
$220 and not worth a fig!' Dad says.
'Try another match,' says Mum.
Dad strikes the match and
WHOOOOOMPHHH!
Instead of a blue cooking flame,
an orange flame shoots high and wide.
Our faces glow
in the sudden blaze.
Dad jumps and yells,
'Quick! Run!
It's going to blow.
Run! Now!'
He reaches for our hands
'Quick!
It'll take the whole camp ground if it blows.
Run!

Run, I tell you.
It'll explode! Run!'
And as Dad is about to turn and run,
dragging us behind,
Mum leans close to the flame
and puffs really hard...

The flame goes out.

Dad is still jumping and yelling,
waving his arms.
'Run! Run!'

Then he sees the flame is out.

The night is perfectly still
not a sound can be heard...
Dad slumps on a camp chair,
and is very quiet for a long time,
until Mum says,
'Let's go to the shop, shall we?
I'd love some fish and chips.'
Dad nods,
'Sure. We'll cook tomorrow.
Let's have a treat for our first night.'

Anna and Beyonce

After school.
I check our house –
no one home.
Mum and Dad at work,
and my brother?
Who knows where Roberto goes?
Time for some secret concert practice.
I switch on Dad's karaoke machine,
search through
a thousand stupid football songs
and another thousand soppy love songs
until I find
Beyonce.
I pick up the microphone,
push play
and start singing
and dancing…
I jump on the lounge,
I slide along the floor,
I even add Sharita's
hip lifts and belly rolls.

Over and over,
playing the same song,
until,
sure enough,
just as I've perfected my
Beyonce bump dance,
I see my stupid brother
grinning at the window.
I bet he's been there for ages
and he looks fit to burst.

I have to get used to an audience.
I know they'll all be watching me,
but Roberto...
stupid crazy Roberto...

I hate him!

Wise things Billy has said this term

When Mr Carey's eyebrows meet,
caterpillars grow nervous.

What's eleven plus seven?
Easy, eleventy-seven.

What happens if you spray Spiderman
with insect repellant?

True happiness can be found
at lunchtime,
when the canteen is open,
and there's no one else in line.

A dead bird can't hurt you,
unless it falls on your head.

Remember, salt on your chips
is better than vinegar on your lips.

Guns don't kill people,
lollipops do.

I can't read poetry,
it hurts my head.

Teachers are like parents,
only different.

Parents are like teachers
that don't get paid.

You shouldn't grumble
if you stumble.

Jason, and parents

I don't understand parents.
When I got detention for fighting
last year,
Dad was so mad.
I couldn't watch television for a week,
as 'extra punishment',
or as Mum said,
'extra reason not to fight again'.
And when I got in trouble for
accidentally
breaking the library window
(how did I know
I could kick a ball that high?)
I had to do special chores
around the house
for two weeks
to help pay for the damage.

So, when they find out
about detention this week,
for kissing Emily,
what do they do?

Nothing.
Not a single thing.
And I catch Dad smiling at me
over dinner.
And Mum doesn't say a word,
except to ask,
'Is Emily that pretty girl
with the dark hair?'
And she starts smiling too.

Peter, in Love?

Do you want a chip?
    She took the whole packet.
Can I carry your bag?
    She filled it full of books.
A double-pass to the movies?
    She took her sister, Angie.
A sip of thickshake?
    She gave me the empty cup.
Help with homework?
    I did it all, alone, late at night.
The secret Sarah told me yesterday?
    She told the whole school.
I offered her my soul, my heart, my hand.
    She said I made her sick.

That night I cried.
The next day
I offered her another thickshake –
with out-of-date milk.
She gulped it down.

Now I really did make her sick!

Billy, in Love?

There's far too much love
going around this class
at the moment.
Emily and Jason,
Mr Carey and his hippie songs,
and now Peter...

What would Johnny Rotten say?
He'd sneer,
swear once or twice,
and start singing a song
about the war,
or being unemployed,
or having a wild haircut.

That's what this class needs:
a good spiky haircut.
I'll ask Dad,
when I get home.

The class respond to Billy's haircut

Cool and sharp.

Like a spiny anteater sitting on his head!

He's ten centimetres taller!

He looks like he's put his finger
in a power point and been electrocuted!

Hey, that's my good friend, Billy.
Some say his hair looks silly
But maybe the barber got drunk
and turned Billy into a punk.

Whatever you do,
don't let him head my soccer ball.

I think the Prime Minister
should spike his hair,
to be just like Billy.

It looks like he's poked
twenty knitting needles in his head.

Billy the Punk rules, okay!

Letter to an author

Dear Author,

I'm writing this because Mr Carey, my teacher,
says we have to.
We like your book.
It was almost as good as *Harry Potter*,
only there weren't any wizards and stuff.
We liked the guinea pig.
We didn't like the principal. He was mean.
Billy asked me to suggest you should write
about football. And ghosts. And goblins too.
Do you have any children?
I have an annoying brother and a pet goldfish
called Max.
Billy says to say that he had a goldfish
called Sid Vicious, but it died.
Do you make lots of money?
Can you put me and Billy in your next book?
Billy wants to be the goblin.

Yours in books,

Anna Baggio (and Billy)

Letter to a rapper

Yo!
I'm Jackson – but call me J-man, bro.
Dis letter for my teacher
he's an education preacher.
Made me write a letter
to a dude who's better.
I thought of you – a rapping man –
cause you can see I'm a rapping fan.
Do you wear a beanie and hip gear?
Cruise with a swagger and have no fear?
That's cool.
You rule.
I wrote a song, you know, a great sound.
A real hot rhythm called
Rappin' in the playground.
I'll post it to you next time, if I can.
Don't forget me bro, I'm the J-man.

I am,

J-man

Concert practice

Anna played a CD
of Beyonce.
She sang all the words
and danced around the classroom.
Billy had shaved his hair,
or as Peter said,
'chased the anteater off his head'.
He played punk double-loud
and drummed the desks in time.
The J-man?
You guessed it.
Rap.
Baggy pants and breakdance,
high-fives and calling Mr Carey, '*Bro!*'
Emily wore her tutu
and butterflied across the room
to classical music.
Mr Carey strummed guitar
and sang in a nasal voice
about dead animals and war,
even though he said the song
was about love and peace.

The Principal sat up the back
and watched the rehearsal.
When the bell rang,
she walked to the foot of the stage,
and said,
'Very dramatic, everyone.
It's coming along nicely.
Well done.'
She turned to leave,
stopped,
and glanced at Billy.
'Interesting haircut, young man.'

The Co-curricular guest

Sarah invited her Great Uncle Bob
to Co-curricular today.
He was very old,
with grey hair,
and a long droopy moustache.
He was dressed in his old army uniform.
He talked about all his friends
who were teenagers,
just like him,
when they went to war.
He talked about the jungle
and the rains that never stopped,
and the two years
in a prisoner-of-war camp,
and how he still can't look in a mirror
without seeing himself as
a bag of bones.
And when it was all over
and the ship docked in Sydney Harbour,

he saw his family waiting
and waving
and he thought of his friends
left in the jungle...
Then Great Uncle Bob
played *The Last Post*
on the bugle
and we all cried,
except Billy.
He sniffled a little
and whispered,
'Punks don't cry.'

Billy and the bugle

I wasn't crying,
anyway.
I had a cold
and forgot my hanky
and Dad said
I shouldn't wipe my nose
on my sleeve.
So I was
sniffing,
not sniffling!
Okay?

Billy? No way!

Yeah,
Billy wasn't crying,
no way!
He probably just
hurt his hands
drumming them on the desks,
before,
when he played his punk music.
Punks don't cry.
Not even with two broken hands.
Punks rule!

Jason

I like Emily.
I really do.
She's smart
and funny
and she's cool to be around,
but
she wants me to perform
in the school concert with her,
as a dancer!
In tights!
She calls them stretch pants,
but they look like tights to me!
I'm supposed to catch her
as she sails across the stage,
and spin her in mid-air
as she raises her hands
like butterfly wings.
Me?
I think I'd rather be Romeo
in a play,
but what can I say?

Every afternoon
as we walk along our street
she pirouettes on the footpath
as she turns into her driveway.
Me,
a dancer?
In tights?
On stage?

And I voted for it!
Jason, the butterfly!

Emily

A concert is better than a play.
I don't have to learn lines,
or act,
or rehearse with the rest of the class.
And I'm sure Jason loves
the chance to be onstage together.
My ballet teacher
says Jason will need lots of practice,
but I'm sure she's exaggerating.
I mean,
he only has to catch me.
Anyone can do that.
And now we can spend
every afternoon together,
just the two of us.
My mum always says
things work out for the best,
and,
for once,
maybe she's right.

The hero of Macbeth

This morning
Class 5P and Class 6C
went to see a play
called *Macbeth*,
written by William Shakespeare.
It's about a bloke with an evil wife
and how they both want to kill
this other poor guy.
It was great.
Lots of blood
and guts
and shouting,
with everyone talking
in a really weird language.

But the highlight
was just before Macbeth
was going to murder the king.
Roberto Baggio
from Year 5
stood up in the front row
and yelled,
'Look out!
The ugly man's going to kill you!'

The actors froze,
dagger raised,
as our whole school
stared at Roberto:
the hero of *Macbeth*.

Anna and the fool of Macbeth

I want to kill him!
Not the king.
My brother!
I swear!
Roberto is sitting right beside me
in the dark theatre
and I'm so involved in the play –
as Macbeth creeps up on the king –
I can hardly stand the suspense.
Will he do it?
Will the king wake in time?

And crazy Roberto
stands up
and shouts
at the top of his voice
and everyone turns
and looks at him
and then
everyone looks at me

as though
I know about it,
as though
I've told him to stand up and shout,
as though
I'm the fool of *Macbeth*!
How could I know
what's going on in my brother's mind?

I need yoga!
I need a whole day of yoga
to calm me down!

Electricity in Anna's house

Tonight, for homework,
we had to study electricity.
Mr Carey told us
to ask our parents to turn off
all the power to our house.

Darkness.

I can hear my heart
instead of the refrigerator.
I can hear the crickets in the garden
instead of my brother's music.
I can see the stars outside
instead of the bedroom light.
I can see the moon rising.
I can hear a bird,
and a dog barking in the distance,
but most of all
when I close my eyes
I can see Mr Carey,
smiling to himself,
and I smile too.

'Right,' says Dad.
'That's enough homework.
Let's watch television.'

Michael watching the weather

When Dad's had a bad day at work,
he brings home a dark cloud
that hovers over dinner.
Stella and me
(thunder, lightning)
sorry, Dad – Stella and I
eat quietly,
politely,
not too much food
mouth closed
chew slowly
don't gulp
sip our water
don't guzzle
ask, 'Can you pass the salt please, Dad?'
Not too much salt,
no thanks to pepper,
elbows off the table,
no wiping your mouth on your sleeve.
All through dinner
we bow under the storm cloud,
wishing for sunshine, not rain.
Then it happens.
I push the peas onto my fork,
slowly,

carefully
lift them to my mouth
and put them all in,
without dropping one.
But before I can chew,
I feel my nose
itching
from the inside.
I'm about to…

Sneeeeeeeeze!

It's raining peas!
Peas on the table.
Peas on the floor.
Peas plopping in the glasses.
And one pea,
one super tomahawk-missile pea
hits Dad smack between the eyes.
Stella ducks for shelter.
Mum covers her face.
And Dad?
(storm? thunder? lightning?)
No.
He rubs his face,
takes a calm deep breath
and says,
 'Great shot, Michael.'

Sarah asks
Mr Jonasforthwalton
three questions

Sir, do you know where the Principal is?
Yes.

Can you tell me where the Principal is?
I certainly can.

Where is the Principal?
Right behind you!

Mr Carey jigged school!

I was eleven.
My friend Brian and I
were walking to school.
It was summer,
not a cloud in the sky.
Brian said,
'Let's go swimming.'
I said,
'We can't. It's a school day.'
'So?' Brian replied.
I never did have an answer for 'So?'
We sneaked home,
got our swimmers and towels,
and raced to the creek,
not far from school.
We swung off the rope
and swam.
It was great.
We lay in the cool shade
and ate our lunch,
and thought of everyone back at school.
Then we heard footsteps...

In the distance we saw our principal
marching down to the creek.
'Quick,' said Brian,
'jump in and we'll swim
to the other side.'
We did.
We scrambled up the opposite bank,
and hid under some bushes.
Perfect.
He'd never see us.
He didn't.
The principal went straight
to our clothes and towels,
on the bank where we'd left them.
He picked them up
and said to the silent bush,
'These will be in my office, gentlemen.
Have a pleasant swim.'
The principal, and our clothes,
returned to school.
Brian looked at me.
I looked at Brian.

That was the first
and last
time I jigged school.

Jason foresees the future

A crowded school hall.
Emily's parents sitting
in the front row,
next to Mum and Dad.
The music starts,
Emily floats across stage
to ripples of applause.
She executes a perfect spin
and tiptoes elegantly
into the centre
with the lights
beaming down brightly
as she smiles at the audience
and prances in ever-widening circles,
gathering speed,
heading to where I'm standing
in black tights
with the words of Peter
echoing in my ear:
'Nice legs, Jason.'

The music reaches a crescendo
as Emily leaps
and flies,
arms outstretched,
as I turn to tell Peter
what I think of him.
And the crowd gasps
as I turn to punch Peter,
whose face is filled with horror...
not because he's afraid of my fists,
but he sees Emily
flying towards me...

Sophia forsees her future

I'll be standing
alone
on stage,
deathly quiet,
everyone expecting
music
and dancing
and wild costumes,
and I'll be up there
reciting
in my loudest voice,
which
is not that loud.
A poem.
A poem I still haven't written.
And you'll be able to hear a pin
d
r
o
p.

And when I finish
they probably won't understand.
They'll think
I've forgotten the next line,
or
I'm taking an extra-long breath,
and
I'll be standing there
alone
alone, with my poem.

The poems Sophia didn't finish

One:

The class sat at their desks
like sheep,
although if a sheep sat on a chair
it would probably fall off
and run out the room
looking for grass
and its sheep friends
in a meadow somewhere.

Two:

The moon glows
like the lightbulb
before my brother
smashed it,
swinging his golf club.
Dad put in a new one
and turned it on
but it still didn't work,
not like the moon,
which works every night,
even without Dad turning it on.

Three:

The day woke like sunshine
then went back to sleep
because it was Saturday
and I didn't have school.

Four:

She was so happy
she purred like a cat
right before getting its tail
stepped on by a blind man.

Five:

He loved her so much
he gave up chewing gum
and eating peas with his knife.
But he kept cracking his knuckles
because he liked the sound.

Class 6C and their favourite birds

'I'll start,' says Mr Carey.
'My favourite bird is a kookaburra.
A bird that laughs.
What more could you ask?'

'And kills snakes too, sir.'

'Mine's a swallow.
Swooping a centimetre from the ground.'

Sarah says,
'A white dove. For peace, sir.'

Billy says,
'I love a cockatoo. A bird with a mohawk!'

'Or a king parrot. A king!'

Emily says,
'A swan, sir. A beautiful floating swan.'

Jason replies,
'A dodo. An extinct bird, sir.'

'A pelican.
So big, and they sit on the beach all day, fishing.'

'A seagull.
He sits on the beach, too, and eats chips!'

'And what's your favourite, Peter?' asks Mr Carey.

Peter smiles, licks his lips, and says,
'A chicken, sir.
With roast potatoes, peas and lots of gravy!'

Windy

Six of us
in the playground
kicking a ball
when
Billy kicks it high,
too high,
and the wind gets it
and it flies
over our heads
and bounces
on the school roof,
not once,
not twice,
but three times,
then it rolls down
over the gutter
and lands
at the feet
of our Principal.

Billy whispers, 'I'm dead!'
Alex: 'We're all dead!'
Jason: 'A week's detention, for sure.'
Peter: 'A letter home. Mum will kill me!'
Me: 'Extra homework. An essay,
or something stupid like that.'
Ahmet: 'That's my ball!'

What does the Principal do?

She puts her foot on the ball,
rolls it back
and in one swift move,
flicks it into the air
and kicks it to us.
She smiles and says,
'It's very windy today, isn't it?'

Mr Holditz

Good morning, Class 6C.
I'm Mr Holditz,
your casual teacher for today.
Yes, Michael,
I know I'm wearing a suit and tie.
And I know that's not exactly casual.
I don't mean casual in clothes,
I mean casual as in...
as in...
I'm your relief teacher for today.
Yes, Sophie,
it is a relief you've got a teacher today
because Mr Carey is sick.
No, not dying, Emily.
He has a bug of some sort.
No. He couldn't kill the bug with flyspray, Billy.
It's not that type of bug.
He is *ill* with a bug.
Sick with the flu.
Not a flying bug, Peter!
Please, Class 6C!

Yes, I guess
we could be Class 6H, today,
if you'd prefer.
H for Holditz.
No, Billy, not
'Holditz by the tail until it barks.'
Class 6H!
And Peter,
Class 6 Spiderman
is certainly not an appropriate name.
Can we get started Class 6C?
I mean Class 6H.

Today, I thought we'd talk about Economics.
Does anyone know anything
about Economics?
No, Anna,
it's not the gym class
your mum goes to on Friday mornings.
And no, we can't do exercise, instead.

Economics means
money, commerce, business.
Yes, Jackson,
I'm sure your dad says
it's no one's business
how much money he makes.

And Peter,
I'm sorry you don't have any money
for lunch.
Well, I suppose
Peter could get a loan from a bank, Sarah,
that's part of Economics.
Peter, sit down, please.
Where do you think you're going?
To the bank for lunch money.
Perhaps I can loan you $2,
would that be suitable, Peter?
Yes, $2.50 is fine.
You can pay me back tomorrow.
What?
Yes, Mr Carey is off for the week,
I'm afraid.
Yes, it was a very big bug, Michael.
No, we can't visit him at home
to squash the bug, Billy.
It's not that sort of bug, remember?

Economics!
Not Health. Not Medicine.
Not Biology. Not Zoology.
Economics!
Yes, Peter, let's make it $3
so you can get a drink as well.

Was that the bell?
It was.
My how time has flown.
Like a bird.
Yes, Michael, like a bug!
No, not like the flying bug that
made Mr Carey sick!
It's not that sort of...

See you after lunch, class.
We'll talk about bugs!

Mr Carey's first day back

Good morning, Class 6C.
It's good to be back.
I'd like to thank you all
for your get-well cards.
They made me feel much better
and I thought the class drawing
of Bob Dylan
was rather lifelike,
right down to his prominent nose
and curly hair.
I'd particularly like to thank
the student who sent me
the can of insect spray
with a note about killing the bug.
Very clever.
He didn't sign his name,
but the spelling revealed
a true sense of originality.
So, thank you,
you know who you are.

And all the class looked at Billy,
who looked out the window,
whistling a quiet tune.

Doodle Alex

Mr Carey saw the doodles
all over my school bag,
and on my exercise books,
and even on my pencil case.
I wasn't sure what he'd say,
but he smiled,
and said,
'Great drawings, Alex.
Lots of character.'
For the rest of class,
he sat at his desk
while we did our
comprehension test.
Every time I looked up,
I'd catch him,
staring out the window,
deep in thought.
Maybe he was still feeling sick?
When the bell rang,
he asked me to stay behind.

That's it.
Trouble for sure,
and all over some stupid doodles.

But he asked me
to forget my homework tonight
and instead
to do some drawings,
simple line drawings
of a few classmates,
and, if I didn't mind,
he'd show them to Ms Park
because he had an idea,
an idea he'd tell me about tomorrow
after he'd looked at the drawings.

Alex the cartoonist

I couldn't wait to get home.
I raced to my room,
got my best pencil
and my art book
and started.
Billy was first.
He's easy —
tall, big, gangly,
with stubbly hair.
I just had to draw Anna
as a dancing pop star.
And the J-man,
rapping,
baggy pants and baseball cap.
Emily and Jason
I drew together,
close together.
I sketched Ahmet
juggling five balls all at once.

And finally,
I did Mr Carey,
only I was careful
not to go overboard
on the big nose
and ponytail.
I drew him playing guitar
standing in front
of this huge peace sign.
I knew he'd like that.

Emily Learns the truth

It was something Peter said.
I couldn't sleep all night
thinking about it.

We were in the school hall,
onstage,
rehearsing for the concert,
and Mr Carey said
it was a dress rehearsal
so I brought my spare tights
for Jason,
and he took an awful long time
to put them on.
Ms Libradore sat at her piano,
calling Jason to come out
from behind the curtain.
And when he plodded across stage,
Peter smirked and said,
'Smart move, Jason.
Voting to wear tights.'

I didn't think about it then.
I was too busy hoping Jason
wouldn't drop me.
But when I got home
and thought about it…

Didn't Jason vote for a play?
For Romeo?

Jason

That's it.
I'm going to punch Peter.
Simple.
I should get detention
for something sensible
like fighting,
not kissing.
And then I'll face Emily.
And I'll try to explain
but something tells me
I've got more chance
of surviving a fight
with Peter,
than with Emily.

Sophia tells

Have you heard?
It's true.
Emily dumped Jason
or
Jason dumped Emily
or
they double-dumped!
They won't look at each other,
or talk.
They won't stand
at the same bus stop,
or in the same line at the canteen.
They sit on opposite sides of the classroom.
When Jason answers wrong
Emily scoffs.
When Emily answers right
Jason scoffs.
They've crossed hearts off their pencil cases.
They both swear
they'll hate each other...
forever.

It's so romantic.

Jason

I hate her.
She's crazy.
She hurt my heart
and my leg.
She kicked my leg.
She missed my heart
but it still hurt.
She doesn't understand.
She thinks she's always right.
I hate her.
It's over.
Never again.
I won't even look at her.
Or talk to her.
Or sit near her on the bus.
No more movies.
No more lunchtimes sharing
Cherry Ripes.
I love chocolate.
I hate her.

Another chance?
Ring her and say I'm sorry?
Ring her and see if she's sorry?
Oh, well…
Maybe tomorrow.
Now?
But I hate her.
Yes, I know I said she was sunshine
yesterday.
Oh, okay.
I'll call her now.
I guess she'd like to apologise…

Emily

Emily walks home,
throws her schoolbag
on the kitchen floor,
ignores the cat,
the chocolate cake on the table,
her baby brother holding an ice-cream,
and says,
'I never ever
want to talk to that
lying
rotten
smelly
slobbery
mean
heartless
careless
stupid
evil
uncool
stinking
worse than brussel sprouts
and

uglier than a hippopotamus
babbling
awful
Jason
again.
Never.
Ever.'

And then, the phone rings…

Jason explains...

It took hours,
well,
ten minutes,
but it seemed like hours
trying to explain to Emily
why I voted for a concert.
I wasn't lying,
like she kept saying –
I just didn't want to be Romeo.

And I think
we're going out again,
because she didn't call me names
and threaten to kick me again,
and she said she'd see me
at the bus stop tomorrow,
and I think everything will be all right,
even though I'm stuck
with dancing at the concert.
But we agreed,
no tights,
just normal pants.
And I'm glad it's worked out.

I'm already preparing for detention
this week,
which will get in the way of rehearsal.
But all this was caused by Peter,
who's going to get punched
first thing tomorrow morning.

Billy saves the day

Jason walks right up to Peter
at the bus stop
and pushes him hard,
so hard
he falls over a little kindy boy.
And Peter
hurts his hand,
landing on the gravel,
and the little boy starts crying,
so I step in between Peter and Jason,
while Michael helps the little kid to his feet.
It seems really weird,
but Jason wants to fight Peter
right in front of everyone
because of something Peter said.
And Alex is holding Jason back,
and no one is holding Peter,
which makes me think that,
maybe,
Peter might like to apologise
for whatever it was he said.

So I suggest that,
and Peter shrugs
and says sorry.
That sounds fine to me,
so I do what my dad taught me.
I look Jason straight in the eye,
and I say,
'He's sorry.
That's enough. Right?'
And Jason looks at me,
and he thinks for a bit.
I can see his brain ticking over,
slow,
like my brain does in Maths,
and Jason shakes hands with Peter,
and they both say sorry again
and it's all over,
except we have to work out
how to get this kindy boy
to stop crying
before a teacher
comes along
and we're all in trouble!

Peter

Yeah.
I guess Jason
had a right to be angry.
But the knucklehead
didn't have to push me over
in front of everyone.

I'm not stupid.
I apologised
and forgot about it.
Teachers always
go on about us calling names
and making each other feel bad
and all that stuff,
so I didn't mind saying sorry.
Maybe teasing Jason
wasn't such a harmless joke.

Alex agrees

I gave Mr Carey the drawings,
first thing this morning.
He said he'd show them
to Ms Park at recess
and he'd talk to me
during lunch,
in the school hall.
I could hardly eat,
I was so nervous.
What was this all about?

At lunch I quietly
entered the hall
to see Mr Carey
standing on the stage, waiting.
He smiled and said,
'Alex, thanks for coming.
Can you answer a simple question?
What am I standing in front of?'
I didn't understand.
Mr Carey was onstage,
there was nothing behind him
but a wall.

So I said,
'Nothing, sir.
A blank wall.'
He grinned.
'Precisely, Alex.
A boring blank bland brick wall,
if you'll pardon the b's!
How can we present a concert
in front of something so uninspiring?'
I was beginning to understand,
so I answered,
'You can't, sir.
We need a backdrop.
But not a boring bland brick backdrop!'
Mr Carey laughed.
'You see my point,
don't you, Alex?
How about you, me and Ms Park
drawing,
no, painting,
a bright, brilliant, beautiful backdrop?'
I loved the idea.
'It would *BE* a pleasure, sir.'

Anna and the Lasting war

It's been a month
since Sarah's Great Uncle Bob
came to school
and played bugle.
But every time
Mr Carey mentions war
and what's happening in the world,
it's like that haunting sound
returns to the room
and lingers,
Michael asked Mr Carey
if we could write a poem
about war
and maybe
the best one
could be read
at the school concert.
Michael said
you can't just have
singing and dancing.
You should have spoken words.

And even though Mr Carey
was a little nervous
about what our parents would say,
he let us write the poems,
and read them aloud,
and vote.
Yes,
a secret ballot,
again.

Anna's poem on World War One

If they called World War One
'the war to end all wars',
what happened?

Peter's war poem

If everybody dies,
how do you know who won?

Billy's war poem

My dad says
that if someone
breaks into his house
and tries to hurt us,
he's going to get really angry
and fight back
and not stop fighting
until they leave us alone,
or the cops come.

Mr Carey's war poem

All around the world
the birds were singing
the salmon swam upstream to spawn
a crab scuttled sideways
on a lonesome beach
enjoying the crazy dance
a dog lazily wagged his tail
as he dozed
under a spreading oak tree
and two butterflies floated
on the warm east breeze
to show us all
how stupid we humans are.

War (a poem by Sophia)

Tanks on dirt roads,
guns firing a deadly echo,
planes swooping low.
Green tracer lines across the night sky.
Noise.
Lots of noise.
And dust,
choking dust
and
and
and
children in hospitals,
their mothers hunched over,
wailing;
and old men
with sad vacant eyes
walking on crutches,
an empty flap where their leg should be.
Bodies by the roadside.
Bodies of ordinary people
and none of them
are wearing uniforms.
They are dressed like you and me.

And our Prime Minister
stands in Parliament
dressed in a suit
with a clean white shirt and tie,
and he has shiny glasses
and he tells us
we need to fight
to help all the people we've seen
in hospitals,
in burnt out buildings,
in old cars fleeing the tanks,
in dusty streets

and
I don't think
we're doing a very good job.

Michael and the winner

Billy put his hand up
as soon as Sophie
finished her poem
and said,
'Sir. I don't think
we need a secret ballot.'
And even though
he didn't mention Sophie,
we all knew what he meant.
So I said,
'Yes, sir.
I reckon we all know
who should read her poem,
don't you?'
And Mr Carey looked around
at each of us in class,
and he smiled
and said,
'Great.
Congratulations, Sophie.'

And we all cheered,
except big strong Billy
who went over and gave Sophie
a huge hug,
and held her hand high,
like a winner.

BiLLy

I didn't mean anything by it.
I really loved her poem,
so I gave her a hug,
and raised her arm,
like they do in
World Championship Wrestling
when Killer Kostassi
spins off the ropes
and lands slam flat
on his opponent for a knock-out.
The referee holds Killer's hand high.
So I did the same for Sophie.

But what worries me is,
on the bus home,
Sophie sat beside me
and talked to me
about poetry!

And you know what's worse?
I kind of enjoyed it.
Talking about poetry!

Maybe I could invent
a new sort of poetry,
with Sophie's help.

Punk poetry?

Anna and the genius

Billy is a genius.

We're all sitting around class
talking to Mr Carey
about how busy we are
with all the rehearsals,
and Sophie is practising
how to perform her poem,
and the J-man's
rapping every night,
and Emily's dancing,
and Jason has joined a gym –
pumping weights so he can catch Emily –
and I'm having a rethink…
Beyonce? Or an original number?
And Ms Libradore
still won't let Billy play punk piano,
and Ahmet is mastering his
soccer ball juggling act,
which the Principal says is
'an insurance question mark',
whatever that means…

when Billy leans back is his chair
and says,
in the most sincere voice
I've ever heard in my life,
'Sir, I'd love to finish
my Maths homework tonight,
but I have to spend all evening
working on my song.'

And Mr Carey laughs,
and says,
'All homework is cancelled
until after the concert.'

Everyone cheers,
and I swear Mr Carey
winks at Billy,
who just keeps grinning
all afternoon.

Love is in the air
(Anna's Latest Secret)

Peter said it's true
and he wouldn't lie,
well, not often, anyway.
He said he saw
Mr Carey and Ms Park,
the Year 5 teacher,
at the movies,
together,
on Saturday.
And they were laughing,
even though the movie wasn't that funny.
Sophie reckons it's marriage.
Sarah reckons they already live together
but Sarah also thought
Mr Carey had a fake beard
when he first arrived,
so I wouldn't believe that.
Billy says his dad says
teachers always marry other teachers
like movie stars marry movie stars
and pop stars marry pop stars.

While we all thought about that,
Michael said,
'No way can they marry.'
'Why?' everyone asked.
'Because of Ms Park.'
'What about Ms Park?'
'Her first name,' said Michael.
'What?'
'It's Sherry!
Sherry Carey!'
Emily suggested Mr Carey
could take Ms Park's name.
'Even worse,' said Michael.
'It's Mark.
Mark Park!'
Mark Park
or Sherry Carey.
The bell rang for class,
and Sarah said,
'Let's hope they
keep living together!'

The Billy poem to end all poems, okay!

There are lots of poems about
streams bubbling along nicely
over rocks and pebbles and
the guggle giggle tinkle pinkle
sound they make.
There's lots of poems like that.
Well, this isn't one of them.

There are lots of poems about Auntie Jean
who knits colourful socks
for her pet goldfish and
talks to the parrot named Pete
who's been dead for months and
she wonders why he doesn't sing.
There's lots of poems like that.
Well, this isn't one of them.

There are lots of poems about food.
Spaghetti on babies' heads
and ice-cream with nuts and
chocolate sprinkles and topping,
yeah, caramel topping, and
a double-crunch cone with maple flavouring.
Yeah, there's lots of poems like that.
Well, this isn't one of them.

My poem is an invisible poem about whales!
Yeah, whales.
It goes like this...

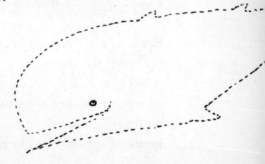

Anna and the big night

We all get to the school hall
really early for our big night.
Everyone is rushing around backstage,
fixing their costumes,
finding the marks on the stage
where they should stand.
Ms Libradore sits at the piano,
humming along as she plays
endless slow ballads.
Ms Park scurries around
adjusting the props
and checking the lights.
Alex is admiring his fantastic backdrop –
an amazing mural of Class 6C.
He's drawn me
dancing and singing and smiling.
I hope it comes true tonight!

Peter stands at the microphone,
repeating the words,
'Check. 1, 2, 3, 4, 79. Check, check.'
Ahmet sits against the wall
with his soccer ball
rolling it slowly, hand to hand.

Sophie stands behind the curtain
with her eyes closed,
mouthing the words to her poem,
over and over.
Mr Carey is super calm.
He sits on his 'director's chair'
beside the stage,
saying softly,
'Don't worry, Class 6C.
Everything will be fine.'
The only time he looks anxious
is when he sees Billy's outfit.
You guessed it:
torn jeans, big boots,
and a mohawk!
Mr Carey says,
'There will be young children
in the audience remember, Billy.'
Billy grins,
'Trust me, sir.
Have I ever let you down?'
Silence hangs in the air
as Mr Carey considers his answer.

Michael and the raffle

Maybe Mr Holditz
and all his talk about Economics
somehow
wore off on me.
I volunteer to sell raffle tickets
before the concert begins.
So I wander among the teachers,
and the parents
who are all talking excitedly
and checking their video cameras,
ready for the big event.
Only problem is I've forgotten
to organise a prize...

So I tell everyone
that Mr Carey
will shave his head
and we'll donate all the money
to charity,
to the Save the Children fund.
I don't know why I said that.
It was the first thing
that popped into my head.
Why would I buy a raffle ticket?
To win a trip to Disneyland,
or to see Mr Carey bald?
Simple.

I can't believe how many tickets I sell!
Billy's dad even offers
to get his shears from home,
and do it onstage tonight.
I reckon I'm the best salesman in school!

J-man Class 6C Rap

Well, yo there! Family,
I'm up here tonight
to bring you Class 6C…

We got Sarah, Michael, Billy and Peter,
who moves so fast you'd swear he was a cheetah.
Don't forget Rachel, Sean and Ahmet,
he's the funkiest ball-juggler, no sweat!
Then there's Jessica, Bella and Emily,
she's a wicked dancer, I think you'll agree.
Wait one second, remember Anna?
She's going to sing a tune to the piana.
So sit right down, stay cool, you can't lose.
Let old Class 6C, entertain youse!

I raise
my arms
gracefull

Emily

I'm not nervous.
Not at all.
I'm not shaking.
It's just a little cold,
so I'm shivering,
standing here
behind the curtain,
in my leotard.
I see Jason
stage right,
ready.
He doesn't look too scared,
but it's hard to tell,
because he has his head in his hands,
and I think I hear him moaning.
Maybe he's just trying
to remember his moves.
That's it.
He's going through each dance step.
He's not groaning,
he's whispering to himself.
He's whispering every move.
What a professional!

Ms Libradore plays piano,
just softly,
as the curtain slowly parts,
and the first people I see
are Mum and Dad
in the front row.
They're beaming
and the crowd starts to applaud
but I haven't done anything yet.
Then I hear my cue,
I raise my arms high,
gracefully,
and pirouette...

Jason

I'm standing in the wings,
holding my head in my hands
and all I can think of
is when I was six years old
and I went to Michael's birthday party
and they had so much food:
chocolates,
lollies,
potato chips,
red cordial – litres of it!
and ice-cream cake
and trifle
with lots of green jelly.
I remember I ate everything.
I stood by the table
for the whole party,
reaching for a new treat every minute.
When Dad came to pick me up,
that's what he had to do –
pick me up!
He carried me to the car
and I've never felt so sick
in my short little life

until now,
when I'm standing here
and I know Emily is looking across,
but I can't raise my head
to smile at her
because if I open my eyes
I'll be sick.
I moan slowly,
in time with the music,
waiting for my cue...

Sophie

It's like I thought it would be.
Absolute silence.
Just me and my poem.
But,
as I stand onstage
preparing to start,
I realise the audience is quiet
because they want to hear me.
Silence isn't scary.
It's like Mr Carey said,
silence is my chance.
And so I speak,
slowly
and clearly,
and I don't see
the faces in front of me.
I see the images of my poem,
and I think only of what I'm saying
and how much it means to me.
My voice grows stronger
and I don't have to struggle
to remember the words.

I know them
because I wrote them.

Ahmet

It's like being in my backyard,
just me and the ball,
with a hundred neighbours watching!
I start on my thigh,
high-stepping around the stage,
my eyes on the ball,
my breath steady,
and then I let it drop to my instep.
This is a breeze.
Hands wide for balance,
counting,
51-52-53-54-55,
and all of a sudden
I hear the audience
gently clapping in time…
in time with my juggling
and it makes it even easier.
I can't stop.
I'm sure I could do this forever.
I'm one with the ball.
Like Mr Carey says at yoga,
'Relax.
Be at peace.'

So this is what he meant…

Billy's surprise

We all expect Billy
to come out screaming,
and yes,
his mohawk looks deadly,
especially with the ragged jeans,
and safety pins everywhere.
I'm sure I see Mr Carey
close his eyes
waiting for the worst,
until we hear
the lone sound of a bugle —
the gentle, haunting,
unforgettable sound of
Sarah's Great Uncle Bob
playing.
He's in uniform,
in the darkness,
offstage,
blowing softly
as Billy plays a single snare drum —

a quiet steady drum-roll,
getting faster, louder,
as the bugle moans behind
and Billy's drum
sounds like distant gunfire
echoing.
Great Uncle Bob
plays so sadly
as he slowly marches onstage
to stand beside Billy,
who plays softer, slower,
so it's like the gunfire is fading,
fading away to nothing.
Then all we hear is the bugle
and Billy stands to attention
with Great Uncle Bob
blowing a final lingering note.

No one makes a sound.
It's a minute's silence.
A perfect silence.

Peter

I couldn't believe it.
Not one mistake.
Jason not only caught Emily,
he spun her in mid-air,
and everyone held their breath,
but Jason wrapped his arms around her,
swaying ever so slightly
in time with the music.
I think he was even smiling.

The J-man shuffled across stage
and did the Class 6C rap.
He finished with a wild breakdance
singing,
'Remember me, I'm free.
I'm J-man, call me Jackson.'

Everyone loved Sophie's poem.
We knew they would.
And Anna sang like a nightingale.
I don't know how a nightingale sings,
but that's what Mr Carey suggested I say.

But I reckon he was wrong, you know,
not because Anna didn't sing well –
she was fantastic.
But a nightingale is a bird,
and Anna didn't sound like a bird.
So instead of saying what Mr Carey told me,
I announced,
'Anna Baggio,
better than Beyonce!'
Mr Carey smiled
and gave me the thumbs-up.
And rumour has it
that Ahmet might be signed up
by the local football team
after his soccer-juggling act.
He can't stop –
he kept juggling the ball
like a crazy seal at a circus.
We had to close the curtain
or he would have gone on forever.

Billy's peace song
touched us all
and Great Uncle Bob
stood proudly

all night, backstage,
watching every performer.
Mr Carey was very pleased
Billy didn't swear once.
And Mr Carey said that the school
is going to keep Alex's mural
as the backdrop for the school stage.

But this is the strange thing.
When I go onstage at the end
to ask everyone,
including Mr Carey,
Ms Park,
and Ms Libradore
to join us for a final bow,
all the audience stand and cheer
and clap –
some even whistle –
and even though I'm only the host
I feel that a little bit,
just a tiny bit,
of all the applause is for me
and the job I've done.

Michael and the first prize

Everything is perfect,
as we take our final bows.
We all join hands,
and bow, time and time again.
The Principal wanders onstage
clapping, smiling
and shaking hands
with Mr C and Ms Park.
Miss Libradore
keeps right on playing the piano
like she's never going to stop.
All the families stand and cheer.
It's the best night of our lives
until
the Principal announces
that the raffle will be drawn
by Billy
as a reward
for the most *interesting* costume.

And the first prize is…

I can see Billy's dad
searching for the twenty tickets
he's stuffed in his pockets.

As Billy reaches in to draw the winning ticket
(and nearly pokes the Principal in the eye
with his mohawk),
I whisper the bad news to Mr Carey.
I keep saying,
'Sorry, sir.
It's for charity.
I'll do detention
every lunchtime
for the rest of the year…'

Mr Carey touches his ponytail,
goes a lighter shade of white,
then sighs,
and says,
'For charity, Michael.
For charity…
And it *will* grow back.
I hope.'

The Principal asks Mr Jonasforthwalton a question

Mr J-F, can you tell Mr Carey
he's wanted on the phone?

Yes. But I don't think he'll fit, dear.

Also by Steven Herrick

For younger readers

The place where planes take off

My life, my love, my lasagne

Poetry, to the rescue

The spangled drongo – winner of the Patricia Wrightson
Prize in the 2000 NSW Premier's Literary Awards

Love poems and leg-spinners

Tom Jones saves the world – shortlisted in the 2003
Children's Book Council of Australia awards

Do-wrong Ron – shortlisted in the 2004 CBC awards

For older readers

Love, ghosts and nose hair – shortlisted in the 1997 CBC
awards and the NSW Premier's Literary awards

A place like this – shortlisted in the 1999 CBC awards,
the NSW Premier's Literary awards, and commended
in the 1998 Victorian Premier's Literary Award

The simple gift – shortlisted in the 2001 CBC awards and
the NSW Premier's Literary awards

By the river – shortlisted in the 2005 CBC awards and
winner of the Ethel Turner Prize in the NSW
Premier's Literary Awards

About the author

Steven Herrick was born in Brisbane, the youngest of seven children. At school, his favourite subject was soccer, and he dreamed of football glory while he worked at various jobs, including fruit picking. Now, he's a full time writer and performs in many schools each year. He loves talking to students and their teachers about stories, poetry, soccer and even golf. *Naked Bunyip Dancing* began as a sequel to *Love poems and leg spinners* but Steven loved the characters so much he expanded the story of their year in Class 6 into a verse novel.

Steven lives in the Blue Mountains with his wife and sons.

www.acay.com.au/~sherrick

Do-wrong Ron

Ron always does the wrong things at the wrong time, or the right things at the wrong time, or the wrong things at the right time... until he finds Charlie, the guinea pig who looks like an oversized rat, and they meet Isabelle, who is waiting for something, *anything*, to happen. When Ron plans a musical welcome for Isabelle's nana, *anything* just might happen... A funny, touching story about a do-wrong boy whose heart is in the right place.

Honour Book, 2004 Children's Book Council of Australia Book of the Year awards for younger readers

By the River

Life for Harry means swimming in Pearce Swamp,
eating chunks of watermelon with his brother and hid
dad, surviving schoolyard battles, and racing through
butterflies in Cowpers Paddock. In his town there's
Linda, who brings him the sweetest-ever orange cake,
and Johnny, whose lightning fists draw blood in a blur,
and there's a mystery that Harry needs to solve before
he can find his way out...An intense story about feeling
the undercurrents, finding solid ground and knowing
when to jump.

Shortlisted, 2005 Children's Book Council of Australia
Book of the Year awards for older readers
Winner, 2005 NSW Premier's Literary Awards,
Ethel Turner Prize for Young People's Literature